AN ORIGIN STORY

Bath • New York • Cologne • Melbourne • Delhi
Hong Kong • Shenzhen • Singapore

MARVEL

Bruce Banner was not always strong.

He was not always powerful.

2

And he was not always able to do incredible things.

But most of all, Bruce was not always feared.

3

In fact, when he was young, Bruce was mostly afraid.

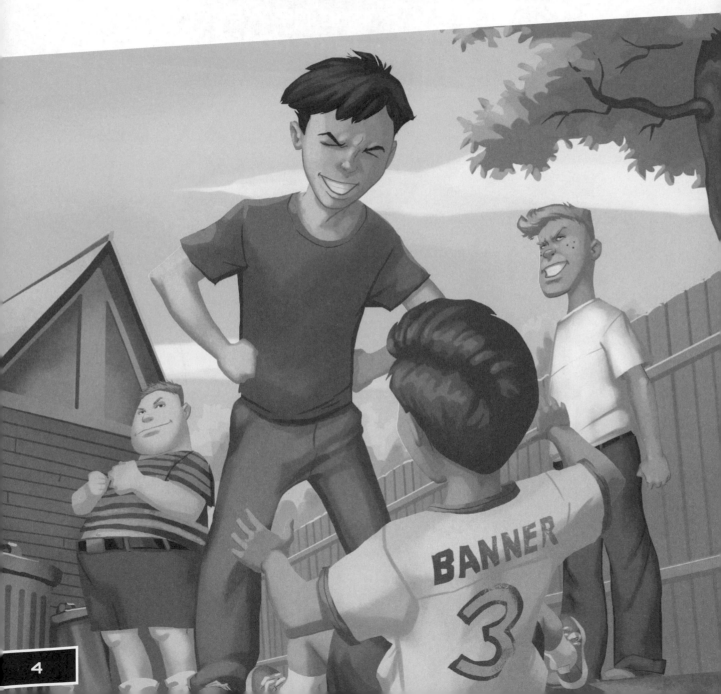

He was often sad and nervous, and he didn't have a lot of friends.
But he was always ready to help someone in need.

Bruce kept all his feelings buried deep inside him. Reading books about science always took his mind off things.

And so, Bruce spent an awful lot of time with those books.

As Bruce grew older he continued to read, study and learn ... but he never understood how to talk about his feelings.

Bruce became a doctor of science who worked for the army. He worked very hard both day and night. He was studying a type of energy called gamma radiation.

It was very dangerous, so he needed to be careful when he was near it. He wanted to find a way to use its power for good.

Bruce decided the best way to test the gamma rays' power was to cause a massive explosion.

He would then measure the dangerous gamma radiation with special equipment.

General 'Thunderbolt' Ross was in charge of the army lab where Bruce worked. He was angry with Bruce. The general had been waiting far too long to find out how much power the gamma rays held. He needed to know right NOW!

But Bruce needed time to make sure the device was safe. He did not want anyone to get hurt. This made General Ross even angrier, and he yelled at Bruce some more.

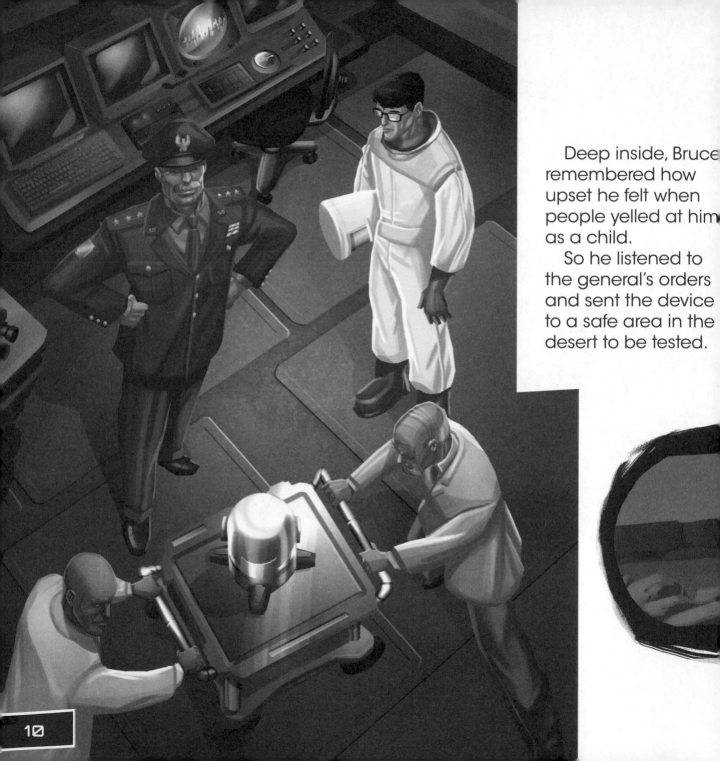

Deep inside, Bruce remembered how upset he felt when people yelled at him as a child.

So he listened to the general's orders and sent the device to a safe area in the desert to be tested.

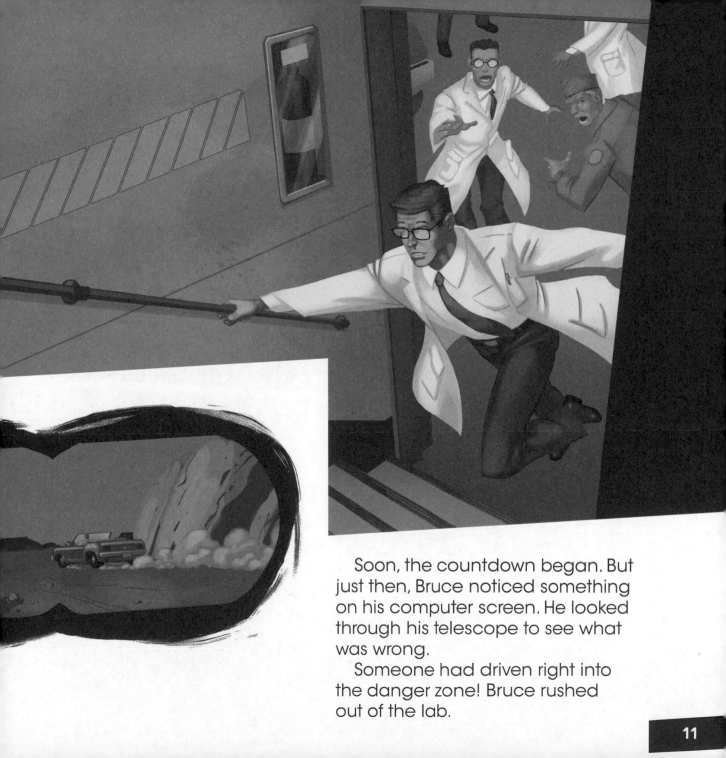

Soon, the countdown began. But just then, Bruce noticed something on his computer screen. He looked through his telescope to see what was wrong.

Someone had driven right into the danger zone! Bruce rushed out of the lab.

He couldn't let anyone be hurt by his experiment. Bruce told the teenager in the car that he needed to leave the site right away.

But Bruce quickly realized they did not have time to clear the area!

He pushed the boy to safety inside a nearby shelter.

SAFE SHELTER

5 ... 4 ... 3 ...

2 ... 1 ...

Bruce woke up in an army hospital.
The teenager was there, too. Bruce learned the boy's name was Rick Jones. Rick thanked Bruce for saving his life.
Bruce was happy that Rick was safe.
He was also happy to be alive.

But, then he looked around. He realized that he was locked up, because he had been exposed to the deadly gamma rays. He remembered the blast. He felt so scared, so confused and so helpless. Just the way he had when he was young. Bruce felt trapped.

And then something changed in Bruce.

The soldiers didn't know that the gamma rays had transformed Bruce! They didn't recognize Bruce. They called him a ...

... HULK!

The army tried to stop the Hulk. But the Hulk just wanted to leave. He didn't want to hurt anyone. He only wanted to be left alone. So when he noticed that his actions put the soldiers in harm's way ...

... Hulk knew he needed to make things right. "HULK SMASH!" he cried.

The Hulk had saved the soldiers and leaped away before he did any more damage.

And not long after, he transformed back into Bruce Banner.
Bruce didn't know if he would ever change into the Hulk again, so he
thought it would be best to hide out and lie low.

All the time, Bruce wondered just how he had become both a mere man and ...

... the Incredible Hulk.